ECHO'S
SONG

written and illustrated
by Beverly Moore

RIVER
WALKER

BOOKS

3334 WYANDOT ST.
DENVER, CO 80211

303/480-5009

RIVER WALKER
STUDIO

BOX 4626
ASPEN, CO 81612

303/963-0582

E
Moore

Publisher's Cataloging in Publication
(Prepared by Quality Books Inc.)

Moore, Beverly J.
   Echo's song / Beverly Moore.
   p. cm.
   SUMMARY: The story of Echo, a cockateel who lives in a
cabin in the Colorado high-country with his family: a ferret,
a golden retriever and a girl. Story tells of Echo's
expressions of his love of life and of his desire to relate to
the wider world of forest and meadow.
   ISBN 0-9637288-7-3
   1. Cockateel-Juvenile fiction. I. Title.
PZ7.M6674Ec 1993   (E)
                    QB193-1072

Printed in USA by Frederic Printing /Denver, Colorado

*This book is dedicated to the extraordinary creatures
who live among us.
They are our teachers and our friends.
They are referred to commonly as "pets."*

In a place high
in the mountains
of Colorado,
there lives a bird
whose name is Echo.
He lives contentedly in
a loghouse with
TWIRP, the ferret,
a yellow dog named TYLER
and a girl
whose name is TRACY.

They live in a cabin tucked in the woods..

. next to a meadow with horses and goats.

Every morning Echo wakes his housemates with a joyful chorus of ROW, ROW, ROW YOUR BOAT... sometimes adding snatches of other favorite tunes.

He has a very special gift. With great concentration and tireless practice.... Echo can copy any sound!

Sometimes he likes to pretend to be the fearsome red rooster....

Sometimes a wise old barn owl.

... and sometimes he just likes to sing in the shower.

At night
when the moon
rises over the trees,
he sings a
silvery moon
song —

Spreads his wings
and dances to a barely
remembered drum song.

Only the mouse
who would come to
his cage every night to
have millet seeds
shares the moon dance.

One lovely summer day the family
went to the meadow for a picnic.

Echo sat very still and listened to the sounds of OUTDOORS. The chatter of the red wing blackbirds on their way to the pond.

The caws of the magpies, the goats bleating

and the horses neighing.

Each time the family
went to the meadow
Echo would listen...
but would not
make a sound.

One day he heard the gentle song
of a single meadowlark.
The song was being sung just to him.

When he got home he thought and thought about the meadowlark's song.

How wonderful it would be if only he could make such a beautiful sound.

Echo worked and practiced in front of his mirror, knowing that the family would again picnic in the meadow and he wanted to sing to the meadowlark.

AT LAST THE DAY CAME!

Tracy, Twirp, Tyler and Echo
went to the meadow for a picnic.

THE GEESE HONKED!
THE MAGPIES QUARRELED.
The starlings zoomed here
and there in tight
formation and even
a hawk circled
above.

WHOA...
WHAT A RUCKUS!

BUT HE KNEW THE TIME
HAD COME.
Shyly ECHO lifted his head
and began his song.
The sound was of life
and wind and sun.

As his heart opened to his world
the sound swelled and
all the birds were still.
The animals looked up from
their grazing.

The song echoed the beauty of the meadowlarks song ....but there was something strangely familiar about the tune .....